D1505493

Go-Kart RUSH

BY JAKE MADDOX

illustrated by Sean Tiffany

text by Anastasia Suen

Chris Kreie
Media Specialist, Eden Prairie Schools, MN
MS in Information Media, St. Cloud State University, MN

Reading Consultant
Mary Evenson
Middle School Teacher, Edina Public Schools, MN
MA in Education, University of Minnesota

STONE ARCH BOOKS
Minneapolis   San Diego

Impact Books are published by Stone Arch Books,
151 Good Counsel Drive, P.O. Box 669,
Mankato, Minnesota 56002
www.stonearchbooks.com

Library of Congress Cataloging-in-Publication Data
Maddox, Jake.
    Go-kart Rush / by Jake Maddox; illustrated by Sean Tiffany.
    p. cm. — (Impact Books. A Jake Maddox sports story)
    Summary: When Tony turns twelve and moves up to the next class
of kart racing, he worries that he will never be able to compete against
the older boys who have more experience.
    ISBN-13: 978-1-59889-320-5 (library binding)
    ISBN-10: 1-59889-320-3 (library binding) 37426862 6/08
    ISBN-13: 978-1-59889-415-8 (paperback)
    ISBN-10: 1-59889-415-3 (paperback)
    [1. Karting—Fiction.] I. Tiffany, Sean, ill. II. Title.
PZ7.M25643Go 2007
[Fic]—dc22   2006027807

Art Director: Heather Kindseth
Graphic Designer: Kay Fraser

1 2 3 4 5 6 12 11 10 09 08 07

TABLE OF CONTENTS

CHAPTER 1

WEIGHING IN

Tony pushed his kart up to the scale. He was second in line for weighing in, after a kid named Devin. It was Tony's first race with his new TAG kart.

He loved his kart — he couldn't help it. The way the red paint was so shiny, and the smooth way it went around curves.

Plus, it was the fastest thing Tony had ever driven.

The thing he didn't love was being twelve. Sure, turning twelve meant he got to drive a TAG kart instead of his old 80cc kart. Sure, the TAG went super fast and looked awesome. He liked it way more than his old kart. But at least in his old kart, Tony knew he was going to win.

Today, he knew he probably wouldn't. And he was really, really nervous.

Tony tried to remind himself how much he loved racing. Ever since his mom and dad had split up, he and his dad had spent every weekend either at the track or working on his kart.

His dad had bought him the TAG kart for his birthday two weeks earlier, and they had spent every minute since then getting it ready for today's race.

Squinting in the hot sun, Tony looked over to the pit, where his dad stood, smiling and talking to other parents. He saw Tony look his way, smiled, and waved at him.

Just then Devin turned around. "Whoa, what is this?" said Devin.

Here it comes, thought Tony. Tony knew the older boys from watching them race for the past few years. They were all fifteen, and they were each a foot taller than Tony was.

"He has a TAG kart," said Jon, who was behind Tony.

"No way," said Devin. "This little kid isn't going to race with us."

"TAG karts only race other TAG karts, Devin," said Corey.

"I know that," Devin said. He rolled his eyes.

"What are you afraid of, a little kid?" Corey asked, smirking at Devin.

"Yeah," said Jon. "Tony here doesn't even reach your shoulder."

"Shut up, Jon. I know that," said Devin. "I'm fifteen and he's, like, nine or ten."

"I'm twelve," said Tony. He was so sick of being short. No one gave you any respect.

"Simmer down, boys," said Larry, the tech guy. "Tony, roll your new TAG kart onto the scale. Let me get a look at this baby."

Tony rolled his kart onto the scale. "Good," said Larry. "It's right on the money." Larry rolled the kart off the scale. "Now let's weigh you."

Tony stepped on the scale and looked down at the number. He smiled, knowing that his helmet, neck brace, and rib protector made it seem like he weighed way more than he did.

"Okay," said Larry. He wrote the number down on his clipboard. "I'll add some weights so you match these other three guys." Larry bent over and put two heavy lead blocks on Tony's kart.

"That's better," said Devin. "We don't want to give him an advantage."

"Yeah, he could pass you up if he was lighter than you," said Jon.

Corey laughed. "Are you worried, Devin?"

"No," said Devin. He reached out to slap Corey. Larry grabbed Devin's arm.

"Save your energy for the race," said Larry. "Now scoot. I have other karts to weigh."

"Okay, okay," said Devin. "I'm going to the pit. See you guys there." He looked over at Tony. "Good luck, shrimp," he said.

It's going to be a long day, thought Tony.

CHAPTER 2

ON THE TRACK

Gently, Tony pressed his foot down onto his kart's accelerator. WHOOSH! The kart responded instantly. He steered onto the race track.

After months of waiting, he was finally on the track with his new TAG kart. It was just a practice run, but still, energy pumped through Tony.

Tony drove from the starting line to the first turn, which was called the Lefty.

At the Lefty, the track made a slow left turn. Just ahead of Tony was another kart. He decided to see if he could pass. Tony stepped on the gas and passed the kart easily.

Then Tony looked back at the driver.

Oh man, he thought. That was Devin. He is not going to like that.

Tony knew from watching Devin race that he hated it when anyone passed him.

Tony turned the kart left as he drove through the Lefty.

Vroom! Devin roared past Tony in the straightaway.

Tony turned left into the Swing Back. This turn went around like a half circle. Tony drove all around the curve.

It was awesome. The kart handled the turn perfectly. There was a straight part of the track after the Swing Back, and after the straightaway was the Hairpin — a really tight, sharp turn.

Tony took a deep breath and carefully turned the steering wheel right as he went into the turn. He felt the kart start to slip off the track, and pulled the steering wheel left. The kart went back onto the pavement.

I better slow down, Tony thought. This kart is way faster than my old one!

Next up was the Double S, two giant S-shaped turns in a row. Tony looked ahead, trying to map out the straightest path through the turns that he could see. He knew he'd never win a race if he ended up off the track.

He eased up on the accelerator and the kart slowed down. On his right, Tony could see Corey coming up behind him.

Vroom! Corey sped past Tony. Jon was right on Corey's tail. Vroom! Jon flew past him too.

Tony followed Jon and Corey on the line. One after the other, they moved through the turns in the straightest line they could drive. Tony realized he'd been holding his breath as he kept the kart on the track. As soon as he reached the straightaway, he relaxed and pressed his foot down on the accelerator. He smiled. His kart could really fly!

Tony turned the kart left again and there was the starting line. One lap down and a whole day of racing to go!

CHAPTER 3

GOOD AND BAD

Tony drove around the last turn and crossed the finish line. He looked at his transponder. He'd made it in record time.

Tony watched the other TAG karts as they all drove back to the pits.

All the other guys would be able to drive for real in a year, when they turned sixteen. And Tony had even seen Devin driving his dad's truck after school one day — his dad was in the truck.

Tony sighed. It wasn't fair. Devin got to practice driving all the time, but Tony had to wait until Saturdays.

Tony drove the kart into its spot and waved at his dad as he walked over.

Tony got out of his kart, reached up, and took off his helmet. His dad gave him a big hug.

"Good driving, champ," said Dad. "That was your fastest time ever."

"But I was slower than the other guys," said Tony.

"It's your first day," said Dad. "You'll learn. Just watch the other guys and see what they do. You'll be the fastest guy before you know it."

Just then, Jon walked past.

"Hey, Tony," he said. "Nice ride. For a while, I thought you were gonna beat me!" He kept heading toward the parking lot. "See ya," he called over his shoulder.

"See ya next week, Jon," Tony yelled back at him.

Dad smiled and put his arm around Tony.

"Let's head out, all right, kiddo?" he said. "I think there's a pizza with our name on it, waiting somewhere."

Sinking into the deep, shiny red booth at Pizzarelli's Pizza, Tony thought about his first day on the track with his kart.

Yeah, it was kind of scary at times, especially when he almost drove off the road. And yeah, the older guys weren't exactly nice to him.

But it hadn't been all bad. He'd gotten to drive his new kart on the track for the first time. He'd gotten to press the accelerator to the floor and feel like his kart was about to fly. That was pretty cool.

His dad sat down at the table carrying a hot, bubbling pizza. "Looks great," Tony said, reaching for a slice.

"I really am proud of how you drove today," his dad said. "I couldn't believe how fast you were out there."

"Thanks, Dad," Tony said with his mouth full. He swallowed and added, "It was pretty fun. I love the kart. It drives so smooth."

"Do you know those other guys?" Dad asked, reaching past Tony for the shaker of pepper flakes.

Tony watched as his dad shook tons of the hot little red pieces on top of the cheese.

"Kind of," Tony answered. "I watched them race last year. The one who won, that's Devin. He's really good. He used to win all the time last year, too."

"Is he the one who you talked to before we left?" Dad asked.

Tony snorted. "No way. That was Jon. Devin doesn't exactly like me."

"Why not?" Dad asked, wiping his mouth with a paper napkin.

Tony shrugged. "Who knows? He just doesn't. He called me 'Shrimp' and asked if I was nine."

Dad laughed. "Oh, man," he said. "People can be mean sometimes, huh?"

Tony nodded.

"Well," Dad went on, "I wouldn't worry about it, Tony. You were great today. That's all that matters."

"I guess," Tony said, digging into another slice of pizza.

"We better get you back to your mom's soon, huh?" Dad said. "Can't wait till next weekend!"

Tony smiled. "Me neither," he said.

CHAPTER 4

IN THE GRASS

The next weekend, Tony sat in his kart, waiting for the race to start. He had qualified for last place. No surprise there. But he wasn't really sad about it. He'd qualified in his fastest time ever.

As he had pulled through the finish line, he looked over to the pit and saw his dad, jumping into the air and screaming with happiness. That was pretty cool.

The track official walked out to the track with the green flag that would start the race. Tony took a deep breath.

As soon as the flag went down, Tony pressed his foot down on the accelerator. The kart roared off!

Devin took the lead again. After him was Corey, and then Jon, and then Tony. Tony squinted, trying to figure out the best strategy. There were eight laps in this race. Maybe there'd be time to pass Jon, and then even edge up to Corey.

Tony followed Jon in the Lefty. Now I'll pass him, he thought. But Jon was driving really close to the edge of the track, and Tony knew he'd lose him if he tried to take the curve on Jon's right. In the Swing Back, it was the same story.

Once again, Jon rode the line right near the edge of the track.

He's following the straightest line! How will I ever pass him? Tony thought, feeling frustrated.

At the Hairpin, Tony wasn't ready. He slid too fast into the tight hairpin turn, too close to the edge. Tony pulled the steering wheel as hard as he could the other way and the kart stayed on the track. Barely.

Tony felt sweat on his forehead. That had been close, too close. And now Jon was way ahead of him. They went through the Double S and were back to the start.

One lap down, seven to go.

Tony pressed his foot down harder on the gas pedal. He knew he could make up some time in the straightaway.

By the time he reached the Lefty again, he was catching up. Around the Swing Back, he was steadily gaining ground on Jon. By the time they went around the Hairpin, Tony was almost on his tail.

One more corner to go. Tony took a deep breath and pushed the gas pedal down. One more corner. Almost around Jon. Their bumpers were almost touching, they were so close.

And then Tony's kart ran off the track and onto the grass.

Tony hit the steering wheel with his gloved hand. He was completely stuck.

Over in the pit, his dad raised his hand, shielding his eyes from the sun so he could see Tony. Tony turned off the motor and waved at his dad.

He wasn't hurt, just embarrassed. He was going to have to sit there, in the grass, for another five laps, while Corey, Devin, and Jon drove around the track, probably laughing at him.

Tony remembered what his dad had said. "Watch the other guys." He'd have plenty of time to do that now.

Tony looked at the other side of the track. Devin had already reached the start and was headed around for another lap.

Tony closed his eyes and rested his head on the steering wheel.

What was he supposed to do when the guys drove by, laughing at him? Was he supposed to pretend like everything was okay? Was he supposed to wave, or what?

Devin, Corey, and Jon roared past. It almost seemed like Jon slowed down, just a tiny bit, as he drove by. He's probably laughing, Tony thought. Great.

CHAPTER 5

COOL DOWN

Tony looked over at the finish line and saw the checkered flag. Finally, the first race was over.

Devin, Corey, and Jon did a cool-down lap, and Devin and Corey drove their karts off the track.

But Jon kept going. He pulled to the side of the track next to Tony, turned off his engine, and took off his helmet. "You okay, Tony?" he asked.

"I didn't crash," Tony said. "Of course I'm fine."

Jon looked hurt. "I know you didn't crash, dude," he said. "Just wanted to make sure you were okay." He pulled his helmet back on, started his kart, and drove off toward the pit.

Tony's dad was walking toward him. He waited for Jon to drive by, then crossed the track.

"Ended up in the grass, huh?" he said gently.

"Yeah," Tony said sadly. "I'm really doing great with my new TAG kart."

Tony's dad laughed. "Thing is, kid, you are doing great. Your times are faster than ever. Every lap is better than the one before it. Give yourself a break!"

"Okay," Tony said. "I mean, I just took that turn too fast."

"That's right," Dad said. "You'll remember that next time. Now, let's get that kart out of the grass and back onto the track, where it belongs."

"Okay," said Tony. They pushed the kart back onto the track.

"Does it still start?" asked Dad.

Tony climbed into the kart and pressed the start button. The engine roared to life.

"Good," said Dad. "See you back at the pit."

"All right, see you there," said Tony. He pulled his helmet on and waited for Dad to cross the track. Then he drove around the rest of the course.

Tony saw Devin and Corey watching him as he drove into the pits. Devin pointed at Tony and then they both laughed.

Yeah, right, Tony thought. Like you've never run onto the grass. Give me a break.

CHAPTER 6

AN INVITATION

At his mom's house the next night, Tony was watching TV when the phone rang. His mom answered and called from the kitchen, "It's for you, Tony."

Tony sighed, slid out of his comfortable chair, and stood up.

He walked to the kitchen and his mom handed him the phone.

"Hello?" he said.

"Hey, Tony," a guy's voice said. It was a familiar voice, but Tony wasn't sure who it was.

"Who is this?" he asked.

The person laughed. "It's Jon," he said. "From TAG."

"Oh, hey, what's up?" Tony said, surprised. Why was Jon calling him?

"Well, I was wondering if you wanted to go out to the track after school one day this week. Just for practice. My uncle is friends with the guy who owns the track, and he lets me go out there during the week sometimes."

"Um . . ." Tony bit his lip.

Was Jon planning on taking him out there and making fun of him or something?

Was this just a chance to get humiliated more than once a week?

"Just you and me, because my uncle's friend doesn't like to have a lot of people out there," Jon added. "I was thinking Wednesday. If your dad can bring you, that is."

"I'll find out," Tony said. "I keep my kart at his place, so I'll call him and ask."

"Cool," Jon said. "It'll be nice to practice with someone besides Corey and Devin. See you in school."

Tony hung up the phone.

"Who was that, honey?" his mom asked. She was standing by the sink, drying a plate.

"Jon, one of the other TAG guys," Tony said. "He wants to practice on Wednesday. Do you think Dad would be able to bring me out to the track?"

"Call him and see," Tony's mom said. "If he's not busy, I'm sure he'll help you."

Tony dialed his dad's number. No one answered, so he left a message on the answering machine.

"Hi, Dad. It's me, Tony," he said. "Um, Jon, from TAG, called. He wants to practice with me on Wednesday at the track. So I was hoping you could bring me and the kart out there. Call me back. Bye!"

"I didn't know you were friends with any of the TAG guys," Tony's mom said when he'd hung up.

Tony shrugged. "Me either. Who knows," he said.

Then he went back to the television. But he couldn't stop wondering. Was Jon really just trying to be nice? Or was he just going to humiliate Tony somehow?

CHAPTER 7

RACE OR DRIVE?

It was Wednesday.

Tony was sure that Jon had invited him to practice as a cover-up for something bad about to happen. But both of their dads were going to be there, so he decided to go for it.

After school, he slung his backpack over his shoulder and headed out to the parking lot, where his dad was supposed to pick him up.

His dad pulled up and said, "Hey, Tony!" as Tony got into the truck.

They drove to his dad's house and loaded the kart into the back of the truck.

When they got to the track, Jon wasn't there yet. Tony put on his gear. Then he checked over his kart, got in, and started it up. He drove to the starting line.

In a matter of minutes, Jon's kart pulled up next to him. Jon leaned over and pulled off his helmet. "Hey, Tony," he said.

"Hey, Jon," Tony said hesitantly.

"Before we get started, I have a question for you. Do you want to race, or drive?" Jon asked.

"What?" Tony replied. "What do you mean?"

Jon smiled. "Well, I've watched you race. You always focus on the driver in front of you, like they're the next turn or something. I was thinking we could just drive. Not try to beat each other, just spin around the track. It's more fun that way."

Tony was confused. "You don't want to race?"

Jon laughed. "Well, I love racing, but it's not exactly good practice. With the pre-finals coming up this weekend, I just need some good driving practice. I don't have my driving permit yet, so I can't practice on a regular car. Corey and Devin both do. That's why I wanted to hang out with you tonight."

"Oh," Tony said thoughtfully. "I see what you mean."

"So," Jon said, pushing his hair out of his face. "You want to drive?"

"Yeah, I do," Tony said. "Let's go!"

They both put their helmets on.

Jon held up his hand, counting to three on his fingers.

When he lifted the third finger, they took off!

When they started, at first Tony couldn't get used to just driving—not racing, just taking it easy and driving down the track.

He kept thinking things like, Okay, if I can get on his left side, instead of thinking about how the track lay and what was coming next and how his kart was reacting.

After one spin around the track, though, he started to see what Jon meant.

When he wasn't concentrating on passing the person in front of him, he could focus on taking the curves at the perfect angle.

He could pay attention to the kart and learn when to accelerate and when to slow down.

Before long, Tony realized that they'd gone around the track six times. Jon started to slow down, and Tony did too.

They both pulled into the pit, where their dads were waiting. As Tony killed his engine, his dad walked over. "Tony, that was amazing!" he said. "That last lap was your fastest time ever!"

Tony felt shocked. "It was?" he asked, surprised. "It didn't seem that fast."

Jon's dad laughed.

"That's because you were actually having a good time driving," Jon's dad said. "That's what I used to do, when I moved up to a new kart: come out and just drive. And that's what Jon did too, when he started TAG."

"And it works!" Jon said.

CHAPTER 8

FASTEST TIME EVER

The rest of the week flew by. The pre-final race was Saturday. If Tony finished in the top three times, he'd make it into the February regional finals. If he made it into the finals, he had a chance of winning a season trophy.

For the first time, Tony thought he had a chance. A week ago, he wouldn't have even thought he'd make it into the pre-finals. Now it seemed possible.

As he drove into the starting grid for the qualifying round, someone called his name.

"Hey, Tony. You sure you're supposed to be at this race?"

Tony turned. It was Corey, smirking at him from his kart. "Yeah, I'm sure," Tony replied.

"Oh," Corey said. He laughed. "Because I'm pretty sure the little kids race later."

Just then, Jon's kart pulled up between them. "Leave him alone, Corey," Jon said. "Tony's cool."

Corey laughed, but then he looked away and put his helmet on. "Whatever," he mumbled.

Devin pulled up alongside Corey, but he didn't say anything.

All four boys stared straight ahead.

The track marshal raised the flag.

And they were off!

Tony pressed down on the accelerator. The engine roared.

Tony raced down the straightaway and into the Lefty. The qualifying race was only five laps, so he knew he had to drive as fast as he could.

Up ahead, Devin roared into the Swing Back. Corey and Jon were right behind him. Tony stayed on Jon's tail.

He tried not to focus on passing, just on driving. But it was hard. The four karts raced down the straightaway.

Tony pulled right to try to pass Jon, but the Hairpin came up too fast.

Jon pulled left to prepare for the turn. They both rolled into the Hairpin.

"Don't even look at the grass!" Tony told himself. He rode through the Hairpin and then straight into the Double S: left, right, left, right.

Round and round the track they went. But when the five laps were over, Jon was still in third and Tony was still in fourth.

Last again! Tony hit the steering wheel. I can't stand it!

Tony drove back to the pit.

His dad was smiling. "What are you so happy about?" Tony asked.

"That was your fastest time ever!" said Dad. "You qualified!"

"Faster than Wednesday?" said Tony.

"Five seconds faster," said Dad. "Chasing those boys is making your time better and better!"

"But I'm still last!" said Tony. "Even though I made it into the pre-final, I am still last."

"For now," said Dad. "But that'll change."

"When?" said Tony.

"That's up to you," said Dad.

CHAPTER 9

THE PRE-FINAL

Tony and Dad worked on the kart until it was time for the pre-final.

When the loudspeaker announced that the race was about to begin, Jon walked over. He and Tony high-fived.

"Good luck out there, Tony," Jon said. "Remember what I said. We're driving, not just racing."

"I know," Tony said. "Thanks. Good luck!"

Then Tony drove the kart out to the starting grid. The grid positions were the same as they had been for the qualifying race. Devin was first, Corey was second, and Jon was third.

Tony was last. All that racing and things were still the same.

The official raised his flag.

Wait for it.

Go! Tony pressed his foot down on the accelerator.

He felt nervous. He knew this was his last — and only — chance to make it to the finals.

The race had fifteen laps. He tried to think about Jon's advice — drive, don't race. Concentrating hard, Tony pushed harder on the accelerator.

All four karts roared down the straightaway. Devin pulled into first. Jon was right on his tail. Then came Corey, and finally, Tony.

Devin pulled into the Lefty. Jon, Corey, and Tony followed him in a line. They were so close together, with hardly any room between their karts!

Tony suddenly knew that it was going to be a very close race.

Jon tried to pull around Devin in the straightaway, but Devin moved over just far enough so that Jon couldn't pass. Then Devin turned into the Swing Back. Jon pulled back behind Devin as they rode around the long turn.

Tony found himself hoping that Jon would win.

Corey unexpectedly moved right to try to pass Jon in the next straightaway. Tony pulled back slightly. He didn't want to spin out or end up in the grass just because Corey was driving crazily.

But Corey had to pull back into the line. In and out of the Hairpin turn they drove, and then they hit the Double S. Left, right, left, right. No one in their right mind tried to pass there!

One more turn and they were back to the start. Devin was still first. Jon was still second. Corey was still third.

And Tony was still last. But he still had fourteen laps to go!

CHAPTER 10

NOW OR NEVER

Round and round they went, lap after lap. The karts were still all close together. Tony was in last place, but he was slowly gaining on the other guys.

Tony came around the final turn and saw the lap marker.

One lap to go.

It was time to get serious.

He pressed down hard on the accelerator.

Tony drove through the Lefty and onto the straightaway. He pulled closer to Corey, but Corey moved right.

Corey was trying to pass Jon. He wanted to move up too!

Jon moved right to block Corey. Corey pulled farther over, but they had reached the Swing Back. Corey pulled behind Jon and went around the Swing Back.

Once they reached the straightaway, Corey tried again to pass. He moved his kart to the right, edging close to Jon's. But once again, Jon blocked him. It was a stalemate.

By the time they were near the Double S, Corey was right on Jon's tail, trying to pass at each turn.

Corey just won't give up, thought Tony.

The track straightened out after the Double S. Corey tried to pass again, but Jon drove right in the middle of the track.

Last turn! Jon pulled left and turned. Corey followed.

Tony could see the finish line. He pushed down the accelerator and gripped the steering wheel as hard as he could.

Ahead of him, Corey pulled to the left to try to pass Jon. Jon pulled even farther left to block him.

They're both on the left! Tony suddenly realized. The right side was clear. It's now or never.

Tony pressed the accelerator down as hard as he could and steered to the right.

His kart roared forward. He could hardly breathe. Slowly, he inched around Corey's kart — and crossed the finish line!

Tony couldn't believe it. He had made it. He had won third place.

His dad came running over, and as soon as Jon got out of his kart, he ran over too.

"Tony! Dude, you made it to finals!" Jon yelled.

Tony's dad couldn't stop smiling.

And neither could Tony.

About the Author

Anastasia Suen is the author of more than seventy books for young people. She has been watching races since she was in elementary school. Anastasia grew up in Florida and now lives with her family in Plano, Texas.

About the Illustrator

When Sean Tiffany was growing up, he lived on a small island off the coast of Maine. Every day, from sixth grade until he graduated from high school, he had to take a boat to get to school. When Sean isn't working on his art, he works on a multimedia project called "OilCan Drive," which combines music and art. He has a pet cactus named Jim.

Glossary

accelerator (ak-SEL-uh-rate-ur)—the gas pedal that makes the kart go faster

chassis (CHASS-ee)—the kart frame

chest protector (CHEST pruh-TEKT-uhr)—a padded shirt worn on top of the racing suit

grid (GRID)—the order in which the karts will race

pit (pit)—the area of the track where the cars are worked on

pole position (POHL puh-ZISH-uhn)—the first spot on the starting grid, next to the pole on the inside of the track

shifter (SHIFT-ur)—a kart with gears to shift, for drivers ages 16 and up

straightaway (STRAYT-uh-way)—the straight part of the track

TAG (TAG)—a Touch And Go kart

transponder (trans-POND-uhr)—a machine mounted on the kart that figures out how fast the kart drove in each lap

MORE ABOUT GO-KARTS

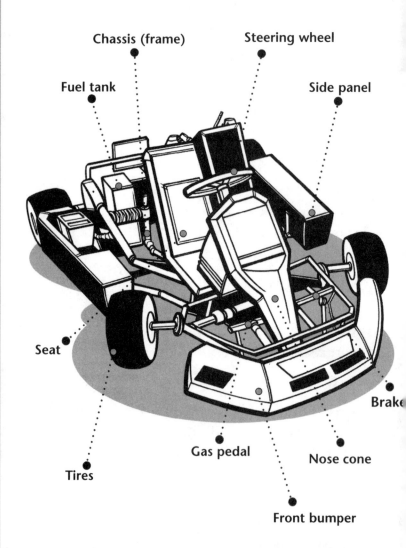

Chassis (frame)

Steering wheel

Fuel tank

Side panel

Seat

Brake

Tires

Gas pedal

Nose cone

Front bumper

Flags and WHAT THEY MEAN

Checkered flag (black and white)—end of race! A winner has crossed the finish line!

Green flag—the race begins!

Black flag—a kart must go to the pit area

Yellow flag—caution; be careful

Red flag—stop the race!

Discussion Questions

1. Do you think Tony did the right thing by moving up to a TAG kart?

2. If you were Tony would you stay with the TAG kart or go back to the smaller karts and win more races?

3. What would you do if you always came in last?

Writing Prompts

1. Write about a day when older kids made fun of you and you couldn't do anything about it. Describe how you would handle the situation.

2. If you were Tony's best friend, what would you tell him to do? Would you tell him to stay in the TAG division, or go back to the smaller ones? How would you help him deal with the older boys?

3. Tony's dad let Tony decide which kart he would drive. Has a grownup ever asked you to make a big decision? What was it? (And if they haven't asked yet, what big decision would you like to make?)

OTHER BOOKS

J A K E   M A D D O X

PAINTBALL BLAST

STONE ARCH *Realistic Fiction*

Max and Tyler have been paintball partners for a long time when they realize that something's strange at the paintball field. A new player in town, Ryan, has just started playing—and winning. At first, Max chalks it up to beginner's luck. But then he starts to notice weird things about Ryan and his team: Can Max and Tyler figure out what's going on before the biggest tournament of the year?

BY JAKE MADDOX

JAKE MADDOX

BOARD REBEL

STONE ARCH *Realistic Fiction*

Tanner Ryan hates everything about his new town. That's until he discovers the Curves, the most amazing place ever to skateboard. Unfortunately, on the same day he finds the Curves, he meets Bennett Parsons III, the resident bully. Can Tanner make friends and still have fun doing what he likes to do? Or has he been doomed to a life without skateboarding?

Internet Sites

Do you want to know more about subjects related to this book? Or are you interested in learning about other topics? Then check out FactHound, a fun, easy way to find Internet sites.

Our investigative staff has already sniffed out great sites for you!

Here's how to use FactHound:

1. Visit *www.facthound.com*

2. Select your grade level.

3. To learn more about subjects related to this book, type in the book's ISBN number: **1598893203**.

4. Click the **Fetch It** button.

FactHound will fetch the best Internet sites for you!